Marigold

Kimberley Johnson

DEDICATION

This book is dedicated to all of those who never gave up on me when I gave up on myself. Thank you for believing in me and holding on to my dream.

"You are never too old to set another goal or to dream a new dream."
-       C.S. Lewis

For all of the Marigolds out there:
Nothing is scarier than taking the first step. Be brave, there is a whole world out there waiting for you.

ACKNOWLEDGMENTS

There are so many people who deserve an acknowledgement here, many of whom have kept me sane, plied me with tea and boosted my confidence when I have doubted myself. I can't possibly list everyone, so I apologise to anyone who doesn't get a mention.

Firstly, thank you to Claire, Hayley, Sheree and the gang. Thank you for being my biggest cheerleaders and listening to me talking about writing even when it has been incredibly boring (most of the time).

Next, Abi, Louisa and Rachael. Thank you for answering a million and one messages when I need a second opinion. Thank you for proof-reading and being honest when what I have written makes absolutely no sense and I have made stupid errors.

Finally, the biggest thanks go to my husband, Matt. Thank you for picking up the slack when I have been too far into the groove to notice that the children haven't been fed. Thank you for constantly providing me with the tea and chocolate I need to keep writing and thank you for giving me the space to explore the worlds I keep inside my head. Thank you for being you xxx

1

Before

The taxi turned the final corner as it made its way along the seemingly endless driveway and the cottage finally loomed into sight. *Home*, Marigold thought. This would be exactly what she needed after the last few months. Some time surrounded by the memories of happier moments while she works out what to do next. She told herself that she wasn't running away, simply taking a few weeks to look after herself, process things and get back on her feet again. Her father had made sure that she had a modest inheritance as well as the cottage before he passed away, so she didn't need to worry about rushing to find a new job, she had time.

After paying the driver with some crumpled notes from her pocket, Marigold heaved her suitcase to the door. There was only one suitcase, there hadn't been very much to pack in her flat when she left and she knew that the cottage would have most of the things that she would need, anything else could be ordered. The door was unlocked with the key she kept hidden under a flowerpot. It probably wasn't the best way to keep the key safe, but nobody ever came out here and it had worked so far. Closing the door behind her and flicking on a light, she looked around and sighed.

Everything was exactly the way she remembered it. The squashy floral sofa still stood in front of the wood burning stove, the battered old coffee table was to one side and reminded her of the time she fell over and cut her eye on the corner of it when she was five, the familiar books were still on a shelf under the staircase and the large windows still offered their view of the garden and the woods beyond.

2

Marigold rolled over and knocked the digital alarm clock from its safe spot on the bedside table, silencing it. She hoped that she hadn't broken it, the poor thing was so old it could almost be considered retro. Slowly, she opened her eyes, blinking at the bright light shining through the bedroom window. She must have forgotten to close the curtains again, not that they ever really blocked out all of the light. She had accidentally shrunk them long ago and now they hung several inches above the windowsill. Of course, ordering new curtains would solve the issue, but they had hung in this little bedroom for as long as Marigold could remember and reminded her of the importance of reading care labels.

Gathering her thoughts, she noted the familiar surroundings of her bedroom. The tired, floral wallpaper, overflowing waste paper bin and cluttered surfaces filled with items that would look meaningless to anyone else; she knew that she should really sort everything out, but it all seemed a little too much like hard work. Sighing, she pulled herself from the warm cocoon of her bed, picked up the alarm clock and pulled on a slightly threadbare robe which had definitely seen better days. Slowly, Marigold made her way to the window, casually running her fingers through her auburn hair in an attempt to brush some of the knots out.

Through the dirty glass, the outside world looked beautiful. Buds were starting to form on the trees within the garden and there were signs of new life forming everywhere. In the flower beds, she could see daffodils starting to flower and the last few crocuses in bloom. Soon, the birds would return and the garden would be filled with song again. Despite the prison that she had built for herself, she never tired of looking through the windows and imagining the world that might still exist out there. If only she was brave enough to take a step outside and find out if her imagined world was anything like the reality.

Years ago, when Marigold had first escaped to this tiny cottage on the edge of the woods, seclusion had been exactly what she had needed. The aftermath of her divorce, unemployment and the death of her father, had meant that the cottage had become a safe space, somewhere that she could pull the broken pieces of herself back together and rebuild whatever was left. Time passed almost imperceptibly here, only noted by the changing seasons or turning of the calendar. But, it had been almost ten years since she had first shut the door on the outside world, she should be healed by now. Instead, she felt just as broken as she had in those early days and rarely ventured any further than her quiet, cottage garden other than for essential visits to the doctor or dentist, which only happened once or twice a year.

On this particular morning, the sun had made its way through the clouds and was peeking through optimistically, offering a day of warmth to encourage the opening notes of Spring. Winter must almost be over, the long months of grey, watery light making way for brighter days and blue skies. It seemed like forever since she had been able to see the sun and feel its warmth on her skin. The little cottage garden was pretty much as far as Marigold allowed herself to go these days, but there were a few lovely spots that were ideal for sitting in a garden chair with a cup of tea and a good book. Maybe she would treat herself to some time outside today. She had read somewhere that vitamin D was good for her, so it made sense to take advantage of such a lovely day.

With a determined grunt, her mind was made up. Turning away from the window, Marigold made her way to the shower, barely glancing in the mirror as she passed it. She knew what she would see there, a fairly average-looking middle-aged woman with piercing blue eyes, who had let herself go a little, or maybe a lot. As she made her way towards the tiny bathroom, she gathered up whatever clothes she could find on her way from the floor; which was where she usually discarded things. There was no need to

put clean washing away, nobody ever saw the inside
of the cottage except for her, and certainly nobody
saw her bedroom.

The shower was cold, as usual, but Marigold
didn't mind too much as it helped to shake those last
feelings of drowsiness and mentally ready herself for
the day. The good thing about living entirely alone
was that time could be spent exactly how she wanted
it. There were no pressures, nobody to tell her what
to do and nothing to force herself to rush for. The only
thing on the agenda for today was her trip to the
garden. With this in mind, Marigold washed her hair
and turned off the water. She knew that her hair
would be wild and frizzy if she allowed it to dry
naturally, but there would be nobody to see it so she
rarely bothered with a hairdryer.

After eating a quick breakfast of toast with jam
and washing her solitary dish in the sink, Marigold
made her way outside and into the garden. The bright
day had formed the sort of determination within her
that was seldom seen nowadays and she was keen
to make the most of it for however long it lasted.

Marigold

It was a fairly typical cottage garden, with
tended flower beds, a well-trimmed lawn and a small
patio area which her parents used to use for hosting
guests when they had barbecues during the summer
months. Marigold used to love it when her parents
held parties; they would always be filled with
interesting people, telling fascinating stories of their
adventures. But that was a very long time ago, a
distant memory of another lifetime. Her mother had
passed away when Marigold was just fifteen and her
father hadn't been able to face the responsibilities of
hosting after that. There used to be a gardener as
well, who would come each week and create the
most stunning flower beds and floral displays, but he
had left when Marigold had moved into the cottage
and instead of taking on someone new, Marigold had
instead decided to teach herself everything she could
about garden maintenance, planting routines and
how to make the most of the space. Now, she had
managed to create a tidy, manageable space which
usually had some form of colour all-year round.

All of the garden furniture was still in storage after the winter, so she had to wrestle a sun lounger from the shed and then find the corresponding cushion. Like everything else in the cottage, the chairs had seen better days, their patterns faded and bleached by the sun. Most of the furniture here was probably older than she was, bought long ago in the early days of her parent's marriage. She had inherited it all along with the cottage and although she knew that some of it would probably be better off in landfill, the sentimental side of her couldn't bear to let anything go. Marigold had left her parents bedroom exactly as it always had been, not even going in there to clean or organise things. When she had moved to the cottage all those years ago, Marigold had moved herself into her old bedroom and shut the door on all of the difficult memories that she didn't want to face.

Finally settling herself in the perfect sunny spot, she set down her mug of tea on the little cast iron table, picked up her book and began to read; quickly losing herself to the magical world of words that had been created. It always amazed her how authors could create literal worlds out of nothing, writing so clearly that the reader could almost imagine that they were there. Today's choice was filled with parallel universes and unlimited possibilities, a fearless heroine and endless power. Marigold's mug of tea was quickly forgotten while she transported herself into the mind of the book's main character and imagined that she too could be just as brave and heroic.

3

All too soon, the tea had gone cold, the chapters of her book had been absorbed and the sun had moved, leaving her shivering in the shade. Heaving herself out of the lounger, Marigold went to move herself to a sunnier spot. There were still a few good hours of sunlight left, so it made sense to make the most of them.

Out of the corner of her eye, she caught a glimpse of something moving. But that was impossible, she was in the most secluded part of the garden, there was nothing but evergreen trees and thick brambles as far as the eye could see. Giving herself a good shake, she bent to pick up the chair and was once again sure that something moved. Something just on the edge of the garden, where the grass met the tangle of impenetrable brambles.

Looking closely, Marigold realised that the brambles were no longer tightly entwined with one another. You would never notice it unless you were really looking, but an almost invisible path seemed to have been cut through the swathe of thorns. She felt a shiver make its way down her spine. The woods that backed on to the cottage garden couldn't be accessed without going through the cottage, nobody ever came out here. Who would cut the brambles and, more importantly, why?

Questions filled her mind as she tried to think back to any time that she may have heard something out of the ordinary; any indication that someone had invaded her sanctuary to cut a path into the woods. But she couldn't think of anything. There had been no strange bumps in the night or unusual occurrences. Everything had seemed completely normal. The cottage sat at the end of a single-lane mud track which meant that it was almost inaccessible during the winter months, being so far off the beaten track meant that visitors were a rarity. The only time that another living soul came near to the cottage was to deliver food or essentials that she had ordered, and they very quickly left again.

Marigold gravitated towards the path, there was something about it which completely fascinated her. Maybe it was the subtle second-hand bravery that she had felt from reading her book or maybe some kind of sixth sense which said that unusual things should be investigated. Whatever it was, something deep inside of her told her that there must be a reason why the path was there and she needed to find out what was on the other side.

Buoyed by her newfound sense of confidence and resolve, Marigold didn't even think to stop and change into more appropriate shoes; the sandals she had come into the garden wearing would just have to do. As she made her first steps onto the path, she was vaguely aware that she could no longer see the cottage garden behind her. It also very quickly became clear that she hadn't realised quite how tall or how thick the bushes were and soon realised that it would be impossible to turn around without scratching her arms and legs to pieces. Regretting her decision to put on jeans and a short-sleeved t-shirt, she carefully made her way through the brambles, trying her best to avoid snagging herself on the brambles and waited to see what would happen when she reached the other side.

It felt as though she had been working her way through the tangle for hours when she finally made it through the bushes, but her watch told her that it had in fact only been a few minutes. Inside the woods, the warmth of the sun had been obscured and it no longer felt like a spring morning and Marigold found herself wishing that she had thought to bring a cardigan. Thankfully, the ground was dry though, so at least she wouldn't end up with muddy toes to go with the goosebumps along her arms and legs.

As she looked around for any obvious reason as to why there would be a path from her garden to this particular part of the woods, there was nothing out of the ordinary that she could see. Trees, mud, fallen branches, that was about it. There was nothing to suggest that this particular grouping of trees was any more important than any other grouping, so maybe the path had been cut through by accident and it was just her mind playing tricks on her.

Gathering her bearings, Marigold decided to give up on her mission and make her way back to the cottage. She turned to where the path was, or where she thought the path should be, and realised that she could no longer find it. There was no indication to say where she had come through or how she could get back to her garden. She must have moved away from it without realising.

Carefully, she tried to retrace her steps, but there seemed to be no sign of a path anywhere, everything looked the same and there was no marker to show where she had come through before, not even footprints in the dirt. Reaching into the pocket of her jeans, Marigold realised that she didn't have her mobile phone, she must have left it on the table with her book and her mug, so she couldn't even check for a map to find her way out.

"Damn it!" Marigold shouted loudly, feeling secretly pleased that nobody was around to see her looking so silly and helplessly lost when she was probably just yards from the safety of her home. Sighing, she realised that she would have to find another way round. There was a path through the trees, hopefully that would lead her somewhere a little clearer so that she could see the way home.

4

The further along the path that Marigold went, the further she felt that she was getting from the garden where she had started. She could no longer see any sign of the edge of the forest, the sun had been completely obscured by dense branches and she could feel the overwhelming dampness of the trees gradually seeping through her skin. Wrapping her arms around her in an attempt to keep the chill away, she stopped to look around. Trees, trees, more trees, there was no way of knowing how far she had come or which direction she should be going. She could be walking around in circles and she would have no way of knowing.

"Maybe I should be marking the path somehow?" she mused while watching a passing squirrel, "How am I going to get home?"

"Maybe you're asking all the wrong questions." The voice came from high up in the trees and made Marigold jump. She was so sure that there was nobody around. She tried to work out where the sound had come from, but there was nothing but trees. Even the squirrel had gone.

"That's it, I'm hearing voices now. I must have finally gone completely mad," she muttered to herself, still not quite convincing herself that the voice had been in her head.

"Try again," the voice said with a chuckle, "if you're mad then I think we both must be. I'm just as real as you are."

Marigold whipped around to where the voice seemed to come from. Directly behind her, sitting on a tree stump, was a little man. She had just come from that direction, so she was completely sure that he hadn't been there before, but he definitely seemed to be there now. A little, old man with a white beard and a fuzzy crop of white hair on his head. There was something about him which seemed almost familiar, as though they had met before. He reminded her of her father somehow, although that was impossible as her father had been a giant of a man, clean shaven, with a head of dark hair which had never greyed. Maybe it was the twinkle in his eyes or the way he sat perched on the stump with one leg crossed over the other, but there was definitely something.

She reached out to touch him, but quickly stopped herself. If her mind had decided to create imaginary old men who spoke to her, then she was pretty sure that her mind would be able to convince her that she could feel him too. Maybe she had fallen over somewhere and was having some sort of concussion-related experience, or maybe she was asleep on the sun lounger in the cottage garden and this was all some sort of really strange dream her brain had concocted thanks to the fantasy novel she was reading. Marigold pinched her arm, hard.

Definitely not asleep, that really hurt and would probably bruise.

"Who are you?" she asked, deciding to play along with whatever mental break her mind had created.

"Always the wrong questions. I think the thing you should be asking is who are *you*?" The little, old man said in a sing-song voice. Marigold couldn't work out if it was just the way he spoke, or perhaps he was taking great amusement out of her predicament.

"Ok then, who am I?"

"Well, if you don't know that, then how am I supposed to know?" the old man seemed to be enjoying himself, but Marigold felt as though she was tying herself in knots and getting no closer to understanding what was going on.

"Why are you here?" she was finally able to form another question, still pinching her arms and trying to convince herself to wake up.

"I'm here because you need me to be. You brought me here because you're lost," he answered with a smile.

"But I'm not lost. My house is just the other side of the woods."

"Maybe your house is, but you don't really know who you are anymore, what you are doing here or where you are going. That makes you lost. I look after the lost things and help them find their way home again."

"So you're here to help me get out of the woods?" Marigold felt a little bit of hope, maybe he could point her back in the direction of the clearing through the brambles. It must be here somewhere. After all, that's how she had gotten into the woods in the first place.

"I can," the old man smiled again, "but maybe you need a little more guidance than that. So many people can't see the wood for the trees these days. They don't even realise quite how lost they are."

"Ok? So what do I need to do?"

"Follow this path here," the man pointed to a path Marigold had failed to notice, "It won't be easy, but that will take you where you need to go. Then you will need to decide."

"Decide what?" Marigold turned back from looking at the path, but the old man was gone again without a trace.

5

After searching around the tree stump for the little, old man, just in case he had hidden somewhere, Marigold decided to take his advice. Even if he was a creation of her concussed mind, her gut instinct told her that he was right and her father had always told her to follow her gut. This was the path she was supposed to take. It seemed a little lighter than the other paths, so that must mean that it led out of the woods.

The path seemed to go on for miles, no matter how far she walked, Marigold didn't seem to be getting any closer to the edge of the woods. She vaguely felt as though she had been going round in circles, but there were no obvious turnings to the left or right and when she looked back, she could no longer see the tree stump or the clearing where the little, old man had sat. She resigned herself to the fact that she didn't really have any choice other than to keep going.

From what she remembered, the woods weren't any more than two or three miles wide so, eventually, she would have to reach the outside again. Marigold's main concern was that she had no way of knowing whether she was going towards or away from the cottage; she had never been particularly good with directions and in theory she could be walking further and further away from home with every step she took.

An hour after she started following the old man's path, Marigold had to stop. The more she walked, the more lost she seemed to be. She longed for the sanctuary of her little cottage garden, her tiny bedroom with the too-short curtains and the security of knowing exactly where she was. She found a fallen tree and sat down, wondering what to do next. If she went back then she would be in exactly the same position that she was to start with. She would still be lost, with no idea how to get home and no way of calling for help. But, if she carried on walking down this path then she could end up even further from where she started and she had no way of knowing where she could end up. Marigold wished that she had never left the garden. If she had stayed there and ignored the brambles, then she could still be sitting and reading her book now while enjoying the last of the afternoon sun.

While she was sitting on the fallen tree, the old man's words started playing around her head again. What was it he had said? So many people can't see the wood for the trees? What could that mean? She looked around her, all she could see was wood and trees. Literally nothing but wood and trees, it was impossible to see anything else. Maybe he had meant something more by it? Surely he wasn't just talking about trees?

Musing on the conversation, another thought came to her. If this was all some sort of hallucination, maybe there was some sort of secret meaning that her subconscious was trying to tell her. She was still partially convinced that this was all a strange dream or mental breakdown. After all, this was real life, not a fairy tale. She might be a damsel in distress, but everyone knew that little, old men don't just appear and disappear out of nowhere. If she could just work out what her mind was trying to tell her, then maybe she would discover that she had been safely asleep on her sun lounger the entire time.

The man had told her that this path would take her where she needed to go, but then she would have to decide, what would she have to decide? Maybe he meant that she would need to decide whether to go home or stay in the woods, but that was an easy decision. Home is where the food is, and the tea, and her warm bed. The woods couldn't offer her shelter or safety in that way. If anything happened to her out here, there was nobody who would notice, nobody to raise the alarm, send out a search party or miss her. Part of her wished that there was someone who would look for her, but then she remembered that it was because of other people that she had taken herself away to the cottage in the first place.

It was something she rarely thought about, but Marigold's mind started to drift back to her early days alone in the cottage. It had been gifted to her parents as a wedding gift before she was born and as a child they had used it as a holiday home. Then, when she had been 34, she had lost her father. Within six months, she had also discovered that her husband was having an affair and had lost her job. It had all been too much to handle, so Marigold found herself escaping to the cottage. When she had first closed the door behind her, it was only meant to be for a few weeks; just while the divorce was finalised and she sorted everything out. Time to recover, put herself back together and decide on what she wanted to do next. But weeks turned into months and months turned into years, until eventually the thought of having to put herself out there in the real world became too much to handle. She was better off alone, safer where she couldn't be hurt by someone else.

Or had the man meant something else when he said that she would go where she needed to go? If this is all in her head, then maybe this was some kind of subconscious spiritual journey where she was supposed to discover the meaning of life and cure all of the world's illnesses. She laughed out loud at the thought that her mind might hold the answer to world peace or some other deep and sought-after question.

Maybe the old man had been talking about a different type of decision, he had said that it would be difficult and there was nothing difficult about choosing between the woods and the cottage. There was only one way to find out though, she had to keep going. Finding the strength to pick herself back up off of the log again and wiping away a stray tear that she hadn't realised she had shed, Marigold found herself walking along the path once more. The trees seemed closer together here and there were more brambles to avoid, she hoped that she wasn't somehow getting deeper into the woods again. Carefully, she made her way through the densest parts of the trees, sticking as close as she could to the path and trying to stay hopeful that this would all be over soon.

6

Finally, she noticed that the woods were getting lighter again. There seemed to be a little more space between the trees and the brambles no longer grabbed at her every time she took a step. Her arms were covered in scratches and she knew that they would sting when she had a shower later. Buoyed by the feeling that she must be getting somewhere, she surged ahead and found herself in a bit of a clearing. It wasn't a proper clearing, not like the one where she had found the old man, but the trees widened out and the path split in two.

There, sitting on another tree stump was the little, old man. Marigold almost laughed at the sight of him and she wondered whether he carried his own tree stumps with him or whether there were just conveniently placed stumps in every clearing. She had no idea how he had made it to the clearing before her as she had definitely not seen anybody else on the path, but here he was.

"Ah! You found me at last. That must mean that you are ready to decide." The man smiled kindly at Marigold, who still had no idea what it was that she needed to decide about.

"I still don't understand what you mean. What is it that I need to decide about? I don't understand," replied Marigold

"Why, which direction you are going to take of course. Isn't that obvious?"

"Well no, not really. I thought the path would show me the way home, but all it has done is make me more lost."

"My dear," the man sighed, "the paths will never make you more lost than you already are, they only show you the way to get from one place to another. Everything else is up to you. But the good news is that you are here now. That means that you have a choice. Are you ready?"

"I just want to get out of the woods," Marigold was close to tears now. Her feet were tired and she couldn't understand the old man's cryptic comments.

"Both of these paths will lead you out of the woods, but you will need to decide which path you want to take. You can go down here," he pointed to the right, "which will take you straight back to your cosy little cottage where you can hide away from the world and never see another living soul for as long as you live. Or, you can go down this one," he pointed to the left, "which will take you out somewhere completely new. I can't promise that either one is without pain, but you are the only one who can decide which one will make you happy."

Marigold looked down both paths. Sure enough, the path on the right looked like it led directly back to her garden. She would almost swear that she could see her garden chair and the table with her book sitting on it, although that should be impossible. It looked familiar and it looked safe. When she looked to the left, she couldn't see where the path led. It went sharply around a corner which meant that she could only see the first few metres of the path. She knew that she should want to go straight back to her cottage, back to her sanctuary where she had created her own little world, but there was something about the path on the left which drew her to it.

"Can I have a moment to decide?" she asked the little, old man, suddenly feeling overwhelmed by the choices on offer.

"Of course, my dear, but you can't wait forever. One way or another, decisions will need to be made. Whatever is lost, must be found."

The cryptic answers meant just as little to Marigold as they had the first time she met the old man, so Marigold found herself a stump and sat down to think. If she went back home then she knew exactly what to expect there. She knew that her days would have routine and she would sit eating her dinner at the little kitchen table; just as she had every day for almost ten years. But, if she took the other path then she had no idea what to expect. She didn't know where she would go or what she would do. She didn't even know where she would live. The thought both terrified and excited her, which came as a massive shock as she had spent so long trying to protect herself from the unknown.

Then she remembered the thought that she'd had while walking along the path. If something happened to her, nobody would know, there was nobody to call for help and nobody to remember her. She considered the reasons why she had originally locked herself away and thought about how that decision had changed things for her over the years between then and now. Maybe her sanctuary wasn't the safe haven she had meant it to be. Maybe she had built walls around herself for too long and instead needed to find people who would care about her if she ever got lost in the woods again. Being alone meant that nobody could hurt you, but it also meant that nobody could care about you. Something in Marigold wanted for there to be someone that cared about her, even if it was just a friend who she occasionally had coffee with.

The old man had been very clear, if she went back to the cottage then life would go back to exactly how it had been before. Her same quiet, little life with her books, her cottage garden and the deliveries of essentials which were usually left on the doorstep. There would be no friends, nobody to care about and nobody to care for. For the first time in a very long time, Marigold wasn't sure that she wanted that anymore. She had thought that being alone was what she needed to allow herself to heal, but maybe she was wrong. Maybe the reason why she felt that she was still broken was because she needed to face the past to be able to move on from it. Emboldened, she knew what she had to do.

"If I go back to my cottage, then I get life back exactly as it is at the moment? Is that right?" she asked the man who had been studying his fingers intently.

"That's right, you get your life in the cottage. Nothing more, nothing less."

"But if I take the other road then I don't know what I'm going to get? It could be something worse?"

"I can't tell you what lies down the other path. I can't tell you whether it will be better or worse than your life as it is right now. Only you can decide that. What I can tell you, though, is that life is what you make it. Nobody can decide things for you." the old man smiled as he answered her questions and Marigold had the feeling that he probably knew more than he let on. He probably knew exactly what was waiting down the left fork for her. He seemed to know an awful lot about everything.

"Ok, I think I know what I want," Marigold said and stood up from her stump. She made her way towards the old man and the fork in the path, "I think I need to stop hiding away and the only way to do that is if I don't know what's coming." She took a step towards the left fork before turning back, "You know, I never even asked your name?"

But the old man was gone. All that was left was the stump that he had been sitting on and a vague feeling that she was being watched. Before she could change her mind, Marigold turned back towards the fork in the path and, with one last glance towards the cottage, determinedly set off along the left fork. It was time to see what else was out there, what lay on the other side of the cottage walls.

7

After

Marigold rolled over and knocked the alarm clock from its safe spot on the bedside table, silencing it. She hoped that she hadn't broken it, she had only bought it a week ago and really needed it so that she could get up for work in the morning. She wasn't even sure why she had set it last night, today was Saturday, there was no work. Slowly, she opened her eyes; blinking at the bright light shining through the bedroom window, she must have forgotten to close the curtains again, they were open wide, letting in the early morning rays which danced on the ceiling.

Gathering her thoughts, she noted the familiar surroundings of her bedroom. The cool cream walls, paintings hanging on the walls and the few trinkets she kept on a shelf above her dressing table so that she could see them and remember the past. Sighing, she pulled herself from the warm cocoon of her bed, picked up the alarm clock and pulled on a warm, pink robe which had been a Christmas gift last year, careful not to wake up the bundle of tabby fur which had been sleeping by her feet.

Slowly, Marigold made her way to the window, casually running her fingers through her auburn hair in an attempt to brush some of the knots out. The windows here were enormous, bringing the outside world almost directly into her bedroom. Through the glass, the outside world looked beautiful. Buds were starting to form on the trees within the garden and there were signs of new life forming everywhere. She had always loved watching the seasons change, but spring meant something special to her. It was spring when she had decided to take back her life. It was spring when she had met James.

A lot had changed since that particular spring day. She had decided to let go of the past once and for all by selling the cottage and had moved somewhere a little closer to town, but not too close as she enjoyed the peace of the countryside. She had found a new job and friends and learned how to be a part of the wider world again. But most importantly, she had let go of the things that had been holding her to the past. The divorce, the lost job and her much-missed father were still a part of her, but the past didn't control her anymore. She could think about those things without needing to hide away from the world.

As if on cue, she could hear clattering in the kitchen and the smells of burnt toast started to drift towards her. James must be cooking breakfast. Marigold took one last look out of the window before heading towards the kitchen to rescue the breakfast and find out what adventures they might be having today. As she turned away, she could have sworn she saw a little old man sitting on a stump next to a nearby tree, but when she turned back he had gone.

ABOUT THE AUTHOR

Kimberley Johnson is a writer and blogger from East Sussex, where she lives with her husband, far too many children and a lurcher called Hendrix. After falling in love with books from a very young age, Kimberley found the magic of creating her own secret worlds out of words. When she isn't typing away, she can usually be found with her nose in a book or exploring the coastal towns near to her home.

Printed in Great Britain
by Amazon

74040948R10031